Wizzbang Wizard

Super Splosh

Finley

Roaring Good Reads will fire the imagination of all young readers – from short stories for children just starting to read on their own, to first chapter books and short novels for confident young readers.

Other exciting titles available in the Roaring Good Read series:

Short, lively stories, with illustrations on every page, for children just starting to read by themselves

The Littlest Dragon series *Margaret Ryan*
The Morris series *Vivian French*

For confident readers, with short chapters and illustrations throughout

The Spider McDrew series *Alan Durant*
The Lilac Peabody series *Annie Dalton*
The Witch-in-Training series *Maeve Friel*

Pants on Fire *Victoria Lloyd*
Mr Skip *Michael Morpurgo*
Daisy May *Jean Ure*
Dazzling Danny *Jean Ure*
Down with the Dirty Danes *Gillian Cross*
The Gargling Gorilla *Margaret Mahy*
King Henry VIII's Shoes *Karen Wallace*
The Witch's Tears *Jenny Nimmo*
Elephant Child *Mary Ellis*

Wizzbang Wizard

Super Splosh

Scoular Anderson

HarperCollins *Children's Books*

For Andrew and Rachel

First published in Great Britain by HarperCollins *Children's Books* 2005
HarperCollins *Children's Books* is a division of HarperCollins*Publishers* Ltd
77-85 Fulham Palace Road, Hammersmith, London W6 8JB

The HarperCollins *Children's Books* website address is
www.harpercollinschildrensbooks.co.uk

1 3 5 7 9 8 6 4 2

Text and illustrations copyright © Scoular Anderson 2005

ISBN-10 0-00-719005-0
ISBN-13 978-0-00-719005-8

The author and illustrator assert the moral right to be
identified as the author and illustrator of the work.

Printed and bound in England by Clays Ltd, St Ives plc

Chapter One

Near the little village of Muddling, at the very end of Lumpy Lane, was a very strange house. Sometimes there were spots on its roof and sometimes there were stripes. Some days the walls were green and some days they changed to blue. Sometimes the house disappeared altogether! For this was Wizard Sneezer's house and it was a magical place to live.

One morning, up in the bathroom, Wizard Sneezer's great nephew, Freddy Frogpurse, was having fun. He filled the bath right to the very top with hot water, stepped into the bath and lay down. The water sploshed over the floor and made a big puddle.

Freddy picked up his wand and twirled it round and round.

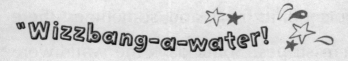

"Wizzbang-a-water!

Stir-up-a-wave!" he cried.

The water in the bath began to shudder and then roll. Round and round went the water and with every sweep of Freddy's wand it rose, higher and higher. Soon, a huge column of water was swirling its way up to the ceiling, splashing the whole bathroom.

There was a flurry of wings as Odds-and-Ends, Uncle Sneezer's house dragon, flew into the room.

"Oh dear! Oh dear!" the dragon puffed, when he saw the water on the floor. "Soggy floorboards again! Now I'll have to use my hot breath to get them dry."

"Don't be such a fusspot, Odds!" Freddy joked. The young wizard was now launching his wand down the bath like a torpedo, trying to catch it with his toes.

"What would your Great Uncle Sneezer say?" asked Odds-and-Ends.

"Great Uncle Sneezer is going to be on his World Wide Wizard Walk for ages," said Freddy. "I'm looking after the house now."

There was a loud thump from downstairs.

"The postman!" said Odds-and-Ends. "I'll fly down."

"But don't breathe through the letterbox," joked Freddy. "The postman doesn't want his hands burnt again!"

"Aha," Freddy said quietly to himself. "Now Odds is out of the way, *I* can make waves again."

He fished up his wand and twirled it round and round again.

"Wizzbang-a-water! Whip-up-the-wave!"

When Odds-and-Ends returned, he had to hover frantically over the bath to get Freddy's attention. Freddy reluctantly lowered his wand and the bath water stopped swirling and bubbling.

"Oh dear!" Odds-and-Ends moaned. "Sodden floorboards, wet wallpaper –

and now this!" In his claws, the dragon held out a rather soggy red envelope.

"It looks official," he added.

"Bother!" said Freddy, looking at the envelope closely. In his head he made a list of what the letter inside might say:

A big bill for all the cakes he had bought in Mrs Muncher's shop – YUM YUM!

A card from his mum and dad asking if he had cleaned his ears and changed his socks – BORING!

A letter from Farmer Tusk complaining that Freddy had turned his sheep into mushrooms – OOPS!

"Whatever it is, I'll read it later," Freddy said, as he jumped out of the bath.

He muttered a few magic words and the towel flew across the room and rubbed him dry. His wizard's gown floated up from the floor and slipped over his shoulders. His hat jumped down from its peg and landed on his head.

Freddy loved spells. He really did want to be a world famous wizard like his Great Uncle Sneezer, but that meant

lots of hard work: learning how to mix
potions; how to recognise plants and
animals; how to use a magic
wand *properly* – and how
not to turn sheep into
mushrooms by
mistake.

No, Freddy liked his *own* spells, especially
the ones that went

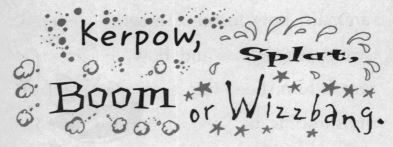

Kerpow, Splat, Boom or Wizzbang.

And he was so busy doing these that
he hadn't even had time to look at
the Wizards' Handbooks that
Great Uncle Sneezer had asked
him to study while he was away.

Freddy called his toothbrush
and it flew across the room,
picking up a dollop of toothpaste
on its way. Odds-and-Ends ducked

just in time as the toothbrush spun into the wall with a smack.

"Oh dear, Master Freddy," steamed Odds-and-Ends, his tail flicking from side to side. "Your Great Uncle Sneezer *always* opened his post as soon as it arrived."

But Freddy was far too busy trying to make the toothbrush come back towards his mouth. It floated in the air just in front of his face. A quick flick and it left a blob of toothpaste on the end of his nose.

"It looks like a very important letter," insisted Odds-and-Ends, tapping Freddy rather sharply on the shoulder. "Look at the logo on the envelope."

Freddy wiped the toothpaste off his nose and took the envelope from the dragon.

"Chief Inspector of Wizards," Freddy read. "What does that mean?"

"Why don't you open it and find out?" said Odds-and-Ends.

Freddy took the envelope and tore it open. Inside, the letter said:

To Freddy Frogpurse,

   It has come to my attention that you have not yet passed your Spelling Test for young wizards. I shall visit you at Wizard's House, Lumpy Lane, on Thursday morning. Please have three spells from the Wizards' Handbook (Volume 1–3) ready to show me.

   Yours sincerely,
Professor Alfonso Blizzard
Chief Inspector of Wizards

The letter sent a shiver down Freddy's spine. In fact, the shiver went right down to his toes and back up to his ears.

"What am I going to do?" he gasped. "I haven't even opened *one* volume of the Wizards' Handbook yet. I'm not ready for a spelling test!"

"And if you fail, then they're sure to send you back home," breathed Odds-and-Ends, trying to get Freddy warm again. "It's Thursday tomorrow. Which means you only have today to learn your spells... and get the house ready!"

Chapter Two

Freddy may not have been ready for his spelling test, but he *was* ready for something.

"First things first, Odds," he said.

"Making everything clean and tidy?"

Odds-and-Ends asked hopefully.

"Breakfast!" Freddy replied. He jumped into his shoes and ran downstairs to the kitchen.

"Do your usual with the fire, please, Odds," he said to the dragon, rather bossily.

Odds blew on the fire with his hot breath and soon the flames were leaping from the logs.

"Do you know what I really love about staying here, learning how to be a wizard?" Freddy asked his dragon. But before Odds-and-Ends could answer, Freddy had picked up a pan and put it on the fire. "You can eat what you want for breakfast *and* play with your food."

He threw some sausages into the pan. When they were sizzling he waved his wand. **"SASSAFORKTASTIC"**, he yelled.

The sausages leapt out, and with another wave of his wand a fork flew off the table and hit the sausage in mid-air.

"Bravo!" Freddy said.

"Watch out!" Odds-and-Ends cried, as the fork flew past a second sausage and narrowly missed his tail.

Next, with another wave of his wand, Freddy sent a piece of bread spinning so fast that it turned into toast in mid-air.

"Oh dear!" Odds-and-Ends steamed, throwing a glass of water over the piece of toast as it burst into flames.

"And now for the orange juice," Freddy announced. ***"SAMBARAMBA!"***

With that, an orange rose off the table and hovered in the air. Slowly, it unpeeled itself to reveal a ball of pure orange juice. Odds-and-Ends wrapped his tail round a glass and zoomed to catch the juice-ball as it fell.

At last, Freddy sat down to eat his favourite breakfast of all: Tingle Toast. He took two large slices of toast and put cheese on one piece and jam on the other. In the middle he put a sliced banana and pickled onions, and finally he finished it off with a dollop of honey.

"Delicious!" Freddy said, chomping his way through his breakfast treat.

As soon as he had finished, he felt another sharp little tap on his shoulder.

"Master Freddy, you won't forget this, will you?" said Odds-and-Ends, waving the red envelope under Freddy's nose. "And before we even start on the spells in the Wizards' Handbook, we must clean your Great Uncle Sneezer's wizard room."

"Why?" said Freddy. "It is clean and tidy, or it was the last time I looked."

Odds-and-Ends shook his head and flapped his wings worriedly. So Freddy got down from the table and marched through to the wizard room. His Great

Uncle Sneezer's workshop was full of everything you could possibly need to be a wizard, from bottles of bats' spit to jars of jellied junipers. Special wizard books lined the walls, with spells on anything from giving people warts to stopping people sleepwalking.

But a thick layer of dust hung over everything. The Wizards' Handbooks that Freddy had to read and learn to become a proper wizard lay unopened. The truth was that Freddy had been so busy having fun with *his* spells that he hadn't been in the wizard room for quite some time.

"Oh bother," said Freddy, throwing himself down on an old armchair. A cloud of dust flew up around him.

"Atishoo!" he sneezed. "I suppose I *should* do some dusting, but I'm sure there's a spell that would do it for me."

He pointed his magic wand at the sofa.

"Wizzbang-a-dust-up! Get-me-a-gust-up!"

he said out loud.

To his delight, the dust rose from the sofa and gathered itself into a little dust ball. He waved his wand at the ball, much as you might draw a picture.

The dust ball formed into any shape he wanted. He made a dust duck, a dust dog and a dust dragon.

"Quack!" said the dust duck.

"Woof!" barked the dust dragon.

Poof! The dust dragon disappeared as a real dragon flew through it.

"Master Freddy!" Odds-and-Ends sneezed. "You're wasting time – as usual."

"I'm only having a bit of fun," Freddy replied.

Odds-and-Ends waved the red envelope in front of Freddy again. Steam was now coming out of the little dragon's ears. "The test is *tomorrow!*" he fumed. "There really isn't time for this."

"You worry too much, Odds. You need a holiday."

"A holiday?" the dragon replied, suspiciously.

"I can manage by myself," Freddy said. "You ought to get out more – make some new friends."

"I'm really not sure that's such a good idea," Odds-and-Ends puffed. "Not many people want dragons as friends."

But Freddy just grabbed a piece of paper and made a list of the creatures Odds-and-Ends could make friends with.

The cats in the village. (Odds-and-Ends had claws and a tail like the cats.)

The crows in the wood. (Odds-and-Ends had wings like the crows.)

The fish in the river. (Odds-and-Ends had scaly skin like the fish.)

"It's time you had a change of air," said Freddy. "We're going out!"

Freddy grabbed Odds-and-Ends – carefully avoiding his breath – and ran out of the house. He carried Odds-and-Ends up Lumpy Lane, through the wood and into the village. He waved to his friends in the village school and carried on to the place where all the cats hang out.

"You'll like the cats," Freddy told his little dragon. "They have claws and a tail just like you, and they love being warm."

"But Master Freddy, the place for a wizard's dragon is in the home," sparked Odds.

"Nonsense! Stay and have some fun!" Freddy insisted. He put Odds-and-Ends down and ran back home.

The cats looked at the dragon and the dragon looked at the cats...

Chapter Three

Freddy ran back to the kitchen of the wizard's house and sat down to eat another round of Tingle Toast. He was just about to take his first bite when he glanced out of the window. He saw

Odds-and-Ends in the distance, flying up Lumpy Lane.

Freddy jumped up from the table and ran to the cupboard in the hall.

"Odds might go back if he can't find me!" Freddy said to himself.

He opened the cupboard door and clambered over crushed wizard hats and broken magic wands.

With a click he shut the door behind him.

A second later there was a loud clatter as Odds-and-Ends came through the dragon-flap in the back door.

"Master Freddy? Master Freddy?" the little dragon called. Freddy held his breath as Odds-and-Ends flew down the hall and stopped for a second outside the cupboard. Freddy felt himself getting rather hot. He'd have to do a cold spell in a minute if Odds carried on breathing outside the cupboard door.

"Master Freddy?" Odds-and-Ends called again, flapping up the stairs.

"Phew!" Freddy whispered to himself. He was pleased to have found such a good hiding place. It was very dark inside the cupboard and Odds-and-Ends didn't suspect a thing. But Freddy could sense that he was not alone.

"Quack!" came a sound from the darkness.

"Woof!" came the response.

The dust duck and the dust dog that he had made earlier had floated into the cupboard beside him. The dog came towards him, wagging its dusty tail. The next moment Freddy's nose was full of dust.

"Atishoo! ATISHOO!" Freddy sneezed loudly, as he fell out of the cupboard and on to the floor.

In a second, Odds-and-Ends was hovering over him, flapping his scaly wings.

"What were you doing in there, Master Freddy?" asked Odds-and-Ends.

Freddy didn't answer. He just grabbed Odds-and-Ends, tucked the little dragon under his arm, went out of the house and headed for the woods.

"It's time to visit the crows," said

Freddy. "You'll like the crows – they fly around just like you."

Freddy left Odds-and-Ends with the crows.

The crows stared at the dragon and the dragon stared at the crows...

chapter Four

When Freddy got back to the house in Lumpy Lane, again, he stopped outside Great Uncle Sneezer's wizard room and peeked inside.

"I suppose I'd better do some work

before the Chief Inspector arrives," he thought to himself. "Odds is right. If I don't pass the test they'll send me back home, and then I'll never be a famous wizard like Great Uncle Sneezer."

He pulled one of the Wizards' Handbooks from the shelves and blew the dust off it. It was called *Simple Curses Volume One: Warts, Spots and Aches.*

Freddy opened the book and looked at a page:

Carbuncle: large boil on end of nose.

Spell 1: Giving carbuncles.

Spell 2: Making carbuncles vanish.

"I know!" thought Freddy. "I'll cast a spell on the Chief Inspector of Wizards so he can't test me!"

Freddy looked at the other books on the shelf.

There was *Simple Curses Volume Two: Laughs, Leaps and Limps.*

Then there was *Simple Curses Volume Three: Snoozes, Sleeps and Snores.*

He pulled Volume Three from the shelf and opened it up. He saw the very spell he was looking for:

How to make someone sleep
a) for half an hour

44

b) for a week

c) for a hundred years

"If the Chief Inspector is asleep for a week then I'll definitely have time to prepare," Freddy thought. He propped the book up on the table, open at the right spell. He read the instructions carefully.

Stage 1: Make a Sack of Sleepiness

Freddy pulled his wand from his belt. He waved it first in one direction and then in another. He flicked the wand and

then twirled it. Next, he gave the wand a little shake. Small sparkling stars danced on the end of his wand. The stars gathered until, at last, a little dark cloud, full of stars, appeared before him.

Stage 2: Position the Sack of Sleepiness

Freddy used his wand to drag the Sack of Sleepiness towards the front door, ready for the Chief Inspector. He was just getting the sack into position when he felt a sharp little tap on his shoulder.

Odds-and-Ends had returned, thrashing his tail and steaming.

"Master Freddy, you're *not* thinking of using that spell on the Chief Inspector of Wizards are you? You'll get into terrible trouble."

"It's quite harmless," said Freddy, making a dive at the little dragon.

"But Professor Blizzard has a terrible temper," said Odds-and-Ends, as he flew out of reach.

Freddy chased Odds-and-Ends round the kitchen, along the hall and up the stairs. The little dragon ducked and dived, zooming up to the ceiling and under the bed, but Freddy just pulled him out by the tail.

Odds-and-Ends was beginning to spark a little, but Freddy just slung the little dragon over his shoulder, went out of the house and down to the river, where he dropped him into the water.

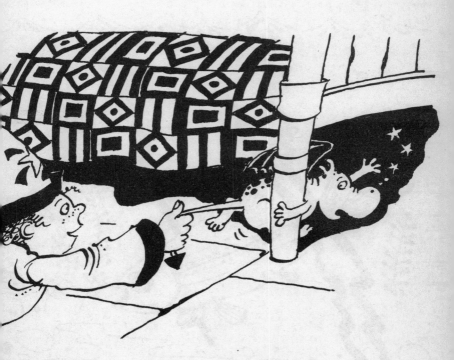

"You'll like the fish!" Freddy said. "They've got scaly skin just like you. And they won't worry a fin about your fiery breath."

Odds-and-Ends floated around for a bit, then held his breath and dived under the water. The fish came to look at the dragon and the dragon stuck his tongue out at the fish...

Meanwhile, Freddy ran back to the wizard's house in Lumpy Lane and shut the door.

He crouched down by the dragon-flap, ready to say "Wizzbang-a-Boo, I fooled you!" to Odds-and-Ends, but the little dragon did not return.

"Perhaps he flew back quicker than me and has sneaked into the Wizard Room," Freddy thought. But when he looked, Odds-and-Ends was nowhere to be seen.

Freddy went round the house, checking every room. There were no telltale burns anywhere, not even a teeny little singe. He looked out of all the windows, peering down towards the river and up in the sky.

There was no sign of the little dragon anywhere.

Freddy sat back at the kitchen table and looked at his Tingle Toast, but he just wasn't hungry any more. It felt quiet in the house without Odds-and-Ends and Freddy didn't like it.

Night fell and it grew dark outside. Odds-and Ends still hadn't returned to the wizard's house.

"Oh dear," thought Freddy. "Perhaps I've gone too far this time. He may never come back."

Freddy felt a horrible sinking feeling in his stomach. For the first time he realised what it was like to be alone in the wizard's

house in Lumpy Lane. It was creepy. He
listened to the sounds of the night. The
floors creaked and the walls groaned.

What had Odds-and-Ends said? "A dragon's place is in the home." It was as if the house missed Odds-and-Ends too.

As he lay in his bed, Freddy worried about the little dragon. *What if Odds-and-Ends is lost? What if he's caught a*

cold? What if he can't even swim?

Freddy drifted off into a restless sleep,
dreaming of spells and dust and dragons...

He was woken by a loud knocking on the front door. A grey morning light streamed in through his bedroom windows and rain fell against the glass. He leapt out of bed, magicked on his clothes and ran downstairs.

"Odds-and-Ends!" he shouted out with relief. "You're back!"

He opened the door – but it wasn't Odds-and-Ends.

It was Professor Blizzard, Chief Inspector of Wizards.

Chapter Five

Freddy was so surprised to see the Chief Inspector that he forgot all about the Sack of Sleepiness. Professor Blizzard snapped his fingers and it flew out of the door and drifted into a field. It hit a cow and the animal fell down in a deep sleep.

Professor Blizzard swept through the door and into the hall.

"I know all the tricks you young wizards get up to!" he snapped.

He went into the Wizard Room and looked around.

"Hrmph!" he grumbled.

He ran his finger through the dust on the table and on the bookshelves and bottles.

"Hrmph!" he said again.

He picked up a jar of bat wings and gave it a shake.

"Hrmph!" he said for a third time. "These look a bit dried out. It doesn't seem as if you've been in here much."

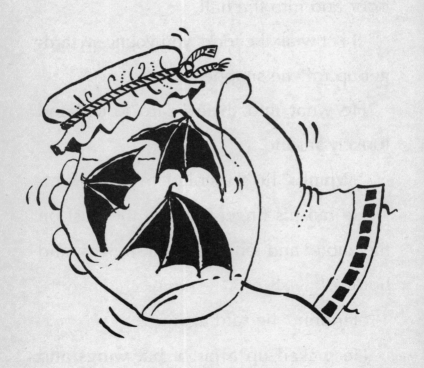

Freddy just stood in silence.

"Well, we'll soon see," said Professor Blizzard. "I will now watch the three spells you have ready for me. And they had better be good!"

But Freddy couldn't think of anything without Odds-and-Ends.

"We have to go down to the village," Freddy said.

"What? Outside again? In this terrible rain?" asked the Professor.

Freddy nodded.

"Well if we must, we must," sighed the Professor.

They walked through the rain, down Lumpy Lane to the village. They trudged

past the village school where Freddy's
friends sat in their warm classroom,
listening to their teacher.

Professor Blizzard huffed and puffed
as he walked, the rain ruining his good
shoes with every soggy step.

Down in the village the cats were sheltering from the rain on window ledges and in doorways. Freddy went up to them. "Have you seen my dragon?" he whispered. "I left him here yesterday."

The cats stared at Freddy for a moment, then one jumped down from the window ledge to the ground. Another cat followed, and then another. One cat jumped on another cat's back. Then another did the same. Soon the acrobat cats had built themselves into a pyramid.

Freddy was as surprised as Professor Blizzard.

The crows looked at Freddy for a moment, then they leapt into the air. They swooped and dived. They flew in lines, then in circles, then in triangles. They flew back to their trees in an arrow formation.

"Caw! Caw! Caw!" they squawked.

"Another piece of nonsense!" Professor
Blizzard snapped. "This is all clever stuff,
but it's not really a proper spell. *And* my
gloves are getting wet!"

They went down to the river. Professor Blizzard's umbrella was leaking and the brim of his hat was filling up with water. "Hurry up!" he bellowed at Freddy.

Freddy crouched down by the river bank. He cupped his hands round his mouth and pushed his face into the cold water.

"Have you seen my dragon?" he called to the fish.

Freddy stood up and wiped his face.

The surface of the water flickered and churned. Then suddenly, first one and

then another fish burst into the air, like a
big fishy fountain.

The fish vanished under the water
again – **Plip! Plop! Splash!** – but
there was still no sign of Odds-and-Ends.

"Hrmph!" said Professor Blizzard, who was now in a very bad temper. "Do you call that magic? Do you call those spells? *I* call that mucking about!"

Freddy thought he had better tell the truth.

"They weren't *my* spells..."

"Of course they weren't," said the Professor. "They were just silly tricks. Anyone can teach a cat or a fish how to do silly tricks."

"...I was just looking for my pet dragon," Freddy added, but Professor Blizzard wasn't listening.

"You were sent to your uncle's house

to learn proper spells!" the Professor thundered. "And another thing. I didn't see you use your wand properly. Not once. Nowadays you young wizards think you can just wiggle your arms around and that will do!

Freddy hung his head.

"I am sorry to say you have failed the test," the Professor announced. "I shall tell the Great Council of Wizards that you should be sent back home!"

And with that, Professor Blizzard turned and marched off towards the bridge over the river.

chapter Six

The rain trickled down the inside of Freddy's wizard gown and filled his boots. His wand hung limply at his side.

"If only I had listened to Odds-and-Ends," Freddy thought. "Now I will never be a famous wizard like Great Uncle Sneezer."

Tears welled in his eyes as he watched the Professor go down to the river to cross the bridge.

But the Professor had just reached the middle of the bridge when something awful happened. The bridge collapsed. The river was so high because of the rain, the force of the water had pushed the bridge over.

Professor Blizzard fell into the water:

Kersplosh!

The Professor was too dazed to save himself with a quick magic spell. He just hung on to his big umbrella as he was swept off down the river.

As Freddy ran along the river bank, trying to keep up with Professor Blizzard, he felt a breath of warm air and a sharp little tap on his shoulder. It was Odds-and-Ends!

"Am I pleased to see you, Odds!"
Freddy beamed. "Where have you been?
I've been lost without you."

"Never mind that!" Odds-and-Ends
gasped, beating his wings so that the rain
splashed all around him. "Aren't you
going to help the Professor?"

"What can I do?" Freddy begged.

"Let's see you do some proper magic!" suggested Odds-and Ends.

"I can't think of anything," moaned Freddy.

"You can do it!" insisted Odds-and-Ends. "Just think harder!"

Freddy closed his eyes, the rain dripping off his nose.

"Of course!" Freddy cried. "The bath! I can use the spell from the bath!"

"*Now* you're talking!" Odds-and-Ends said, letting a little wisp of smoke curl out of his mouth.

Freddy pulled his wand from his belt and twirled it in the air.

"Wizzbang-a-water, Give-me-a-wave!"

The water on the surface of the river began to shudder and then roll.

Professor Blizzard stopped racing downriver.

Round and round went the water, with every sweep of Freddy's wand. Professor

Blizzard went round with it, swirling in a circle, faster and faster.

The water rose, higher and higher, until at last a huge column of water was swirling its way up in the air. With a flick of Freddy's wrist, the column fell in a wave and threw Professor Blizzard on to the bank beside him.

Professor Blizzard's clothes clung to his skin. His hat had been swept away and his beard was soaked.

He opened his mouth and stuck out his tongue, where a little fish flipped and flopped. The wizard picked the fish up by its tail and dropped it back into the river.

Freddy helped Professor Blizzard up and took him back to the wizard's house at the very end of Lumpy Lane. The young wizard sat the old Professor down in front of the fire to dry.

"Well, I see you can cast a proper magic spell when you need to," said the Professor. "But I'm still not convinced that you have worked hard enough to deserve—"

The Professor stopped. He was staring, open mouthed, at Freddy's breakfast from the day before.

"What now?" Freddy thought.

"Is that what I think it is?" the Professor asked.

"I call it—" Freddy started.

"TINGLE TOAST!" the Professor boomed. "I haven't eaten Tingle Toast since I was a boy!"

"Would you like some?" Freddy asked.

"I certainly would!" exclaimed Professor Blizzard. He took a big bite of the toast. As he

chewed he

closed

his eyes

and a

big smile

spread

across his face.

"Delicious!" he said, spitting crumbs everywhere.

Freddy made the Professor fresh Tingle Toast – three helpings in all.

Before Professor Blizzard left the house he gave Freddy an award.

"What's this?" Freddy asked. "A medal for my spells?"

"Don't be silly," the Professor chuckled. "It's a medal for your Tingle Toast! But don't worry – I won't be sending you home now. Your spell to get me out of the river was quick thinking – you've obviously been doing plenty of your own spells even if you haven't studied any of the Wizards' Handbook. You're just like your Great Uncle Sneezer, always wanting to do your own thing!"

Freddy blushed with pride at this compliment.

When he was ready, Professor Blizzard went down to the river and cast a very grand spell to build a new bridge. As he crossed the bridge, the Professor gave

Freddy a cheery wave.

Odds-and-Ends hovered at Freddy's side. "One day, if you do your homework, you'll be able to cast spells like that," the little dragon huffed, as they watched Professor Blizzard go.

"Perhaps," said Freddy. "But sometimes there are more important things than spells, Odds. I'm glad you came back, I couldn't have managed without you. I'm sorry I threw you out of the house – even though you do fuss too much."

Odds-and-Ends wiggled his ears and blew a little puff of smoke through his nose, which was his way of laughing. "I was only trying to help. Remember – a dragon's place is in the home!"

"Well, let's *go* home then," said Freddy Frogpurse. "And make some more magic!"

Don't miss more magical adventures in...

Wizzbang Wizard

Bubble Trouble

Freddy pulled out his bottle of bubble mixture and blew a really enormous bubble. Then he waved his wand...

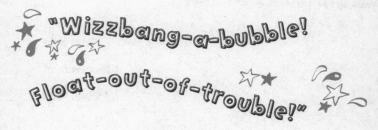

"Wizzbang-a-bubble!

Float-out-of-trouble!"

When Freddy Frogpurse pretends to be his Great Uncle Sneezer, he finds himself in all sorts of trouble. It's time for a very special spell indeed...

0-00-719006-9
www.harpercollins.co.uk

HarperCollins *Children's Books*